Jan Sargeant lives in a ▁▁▁ village in West Yorkshire. Having retired in 2016, she is a successful artist as well as writer, seeing both as helping her live with the progressive disability caused by Parkinson's Disease. Emeritus Poetry Editor for the Quiver, based in USA, she is a published poet and academic writer as well as a house artist for People and Paintings Gallery, New York. In her spare time, she runs a support group for 2000+ others living with Parkinson's and makes banana cake.

Dedicated to my wonderful husband, Ted Kennedy, for all his love, support and encouragement.

Special thanks to Ian Davison – for that throwaway comment which inspired all this.

In lasting and loving tribute to all the members of the Parkinson's in the UK: Stronger Together group, whose support helps us all live with this progressively disabling and incurable disease, whose courage is without limit and sense of humour undiminished.

Jan Sargeant

ALAN'S LESSWILLING CHRONICLES: THE MONOLOGUES OF AN UNHAPPY MAN

AUSTIN MACAULEY PUBLISHERS™

LONDON • CAMBRIDGE • NEW YORK • SHARJAH

A CIP catalogue record for this title is available from the British Library.

ISBN 9781035815920 (Paperback)
ISBN 9781035815937 (ePub e-book)

www.austinmacauley.com

First Published 2023
Austin Macauley Publishers Ltd®
1 Canada Square
Canary Wharf
London
E14 5AA

I would like to thank Austin Macauley Publishers for their trust and faith – in accepting and publishing this book and for all their support and guidance through the process.

Part 1

So that bloke I were on about who bought next door…… He's moved in now with his posh radiators and chalk painted furniture, plans for a chicken sanctuary and God knows what else. Wants to put an herbaceous island in the middle of the lawn. An island! Not a border. An island. Told me bedding was out, perennials were the future and he's even got rid of the gnomes so he can build a small pond. Trouble with men like him, he's not satisfied unless he's ripping up perfectly good lawns and thinking he's Monty Bloody Don.

We've never had an herbaceous in the middle of a lawn in this village ever; nearest we've had to that sort of thing was when that family moved into number ten and put down AstroTurf for the dog to pee on. The Lesswilling village association weren't at all happy about that – we both wrote letters. Plastic lawns are ok in places like Milton Keynes, but we have real grass here in Lesswilling.

I heard them in the garden earlier, too, and he's on about having a new kitchen put in. A whole new kitchen, mind you, not just a cooker or a fridge. We've had our kitchen since before we moved in 39 years ago and it's only ever needed a lick of paint over the walls twice since then; although we had to replace the fridge three year ago when the Sellotape fell off.

I said we could still prop the door up but wife insisted on a new one and said I was making her menopause worse by arguing. And now she's run off with that Farrow and Ball man and she doesn't even want the fridge. Says she's got an American beast. I told her we live in Lesswilling not bloody Dallas.

It's men like him, next door, that turn women's heads with promises of new bathroom suites. Well, you just wait and see and I'll be right in the end – there'll be a Sunday Times supplement saying avocado is back. Mark my words. And then he'll be sorry he put in all that white stuff. And who needs a bidet in Lesswilling? We know how to wipe our arses up here.

I'd write to the council again but my internet is playing up. If I log in, I keep getting that scene in Terminator 2 where all you can see is Arnie's thumb sticking up. I asked next door if he knew what was up with it and he just laughed and said "hasty La vista" or something.

Wouldn't mind but he used to work in IT, wife told me. It used to be so nice here in Lesswilling before he moved in next door. The Co-op shut down last week and there's talk the Post Office will be closed for lunch from next month. When my mother ran that, it was open from 6 in the morning for the dailies, like, till 6 at night. No lunch break for her – unless you count a brawn butty behind the counter. That and the gin.

Ps: Wife just rung me and said the American beast isn't from Dallas and he's not even a fridge. He's from Knoxville, Tennessee.

Part 2

So, all I said to that bloke next door was "If you put that shed there, it'll take light off the lupins" and he got all huffy. He said he would put it where he wanted, and it's not a shed, it's a summer house. A summer house! I ask you, who needs a summer house in Lesswilling? Next thing will be hot tubs and a gazebo and one of them gas barbecues and more fancy London ideas. We have baths in the bathroom up here not in the bloody garden. We buy a cheap throwaway when we want to burn our sausages and we have sheds.

The wife bought me a shed a few years ago, said we both needed a bit of space and I could keep my train set in there. I spent many happy hours in that shed; I once built an entire scale model of St Pancras – the original one before Eurostar and that champagne bar the wife was always on about going to. I told her no way was I going to London to pay over the odds for a drink in a railway station. Not when Lidl were selling Cava for £3.75 a bottle. I thought she'd taken it quite well until she picked up the hammer. She told me that started her menopause off. I was just relieved she'd missed my Flying Scotsman and suggested she ask the doctor about that TNT stuff. Well, that didn't go down well either. It was worth a few bob that Flying Scotsman.

It was around that time she decided to get the Farrow and Ball man in to redecorate the bedroom. She thought it was looking a bit faded after 23 years. I said I'd hunt out the Dulux magnolia from the garage but she was adamant she wanted Elephant's breath. So he turns up with his fifty shades of God knows what and before I know it, I've got paint charts all over the bedroom and then one day, she comes downstairs with a bag and says she's leaving me for him. Says she needs excitement in her life and a pensioners' special at the garden centre didn't really satisfy her – and neither did I. Told me she'd always hated Dulux magnolia. I offered to try Crown instead but she said it was too little, too late.

So anyway, she's now living with him just outside Morewilling, on that new estate. I asked her the other day what was the attraction of a four-bedroom executive detached with electric gates when we had a perfectly good bungalow which took less cleaning. She said they had a cleaner and they'd turned one bedroom into a mini gym and another had a sound surround 78 inch screen with a bar. This is the woman who used to get drunk on a Cherry B when I first met her. Now she's got wine on tap and her own cocktail shaker. She calls him Chuck and he's from Knoxville.

I still haven't got the computer working properly yet, either. All I can get now is that nude wrestling scene from Women in Love. The wife read that with her reading group. They did a lot of reading. Four times a week, they met. Same book for two years. It was longer than the film, she said. I offered to go with her once but she reckoned I'd not be able to understand the dynamics of the relationship between Gerald and Alan Bates and she didn't want me asking any more daft questions, like why would a working-class family from near Nottingham call their kids Gudrun and Ursula. She said I had no poetry in my soul and I could get my own tea ready that night.

Anyway, time for a ginger nut and a nice cuppa before I prune the privet. I prune it every two weeks in summer. On Tuesdays. The wife says they're getting a gardener in for theirs. She wanted one here a few years ago but like I said, why bother paying money for someone to trim your bushes when you can do it yourself. She said it was always better with a well-oiled tool so I bought some WD40, then she said the smell gave her a headache. I thought it might have been the wine the night before. They like a drink at their book club. She told me there was more to life than a sweet sherry at Christmas and a Babycham at New Year. I wouldn't know, I only ever had half a bitter shandy. Dad was a Methodist. Mam wasn't.

She's the one who ran the post office. Before she ran off with the insurance man.

Part 3

Well, I've seen everything now. The bloke next door pays for his shopping to be delivered in a van. Pays for it! I know folk have washing machines delivered, but tins of beans! Why in God's name does anyone want somebody else picking through their plums? The Co-op did us for years with no problem. It's folks like him next door that get local shops shut down.

Got to drive 15 minutes to get to a supermarket now. The Micra's nearly doubled its mileage in just two months. Plus wear and tear. It will need new tyres at this rate. Never needed new tyres in 27 years.

Don't get me wrong. I can see why you might need a new washer delivered. The wife always wanted one of those automatic things. Like I said though, they're not that automatic. You still have to put the clothes in and take them out. And do the ironing. That's not automatic, is it? We've been very fortunate – our twin tub has lasted us since we were married. Bought it on HP 39 years ago and it's been a Godsend. Spinner hasn't worked for the last eight years but you can wring them out by hand. The wife says Chuck has a turbo and you can turn it on with your phone when you're out and about. Well, I rang BT but they said I'd need a smart phone. I asked if a push button one would be smarter than the dial one we have and the man at the other end told me to stop pissing about and get a life.

The wife weren't too keen on the Micra either. Always saying we should look for a new car. Told me Chuck drives a Teflon or something. Electric. But who wants a car with a bloody big plug, eh? And what happens if the lead can't stretch to the kitchen or the fuses blow? Besides, I'm very fond of the Micra. I took it shopping every Saturday, washed it every Sunday morning and gave it a little run out in the afternoon. If it weren't raining. The wife asked me once if we could go for a day trip to Filey but it would have meant motorways. I'm not keen on motorways and I weren't sure the Micra was either. I never took it above 40.

I don't know why he needs food delivered anyway. Wine seems to be his staple diet. You can hear him clinking to his bins. I still remember a time when a bottle of Lambrusco was all you could get. That or Mateus Rose. My mother was partial to Lambrusco. She said it went better with the butties than the gin at lunchtime. Or maybe it was with the gin. She stopped putting brown sauce on her butties, I know that. Next door said he has a vineyard in France. I said he could put his name down for an allotment up here instead. He said he'd rather have grapes than carrots. I told him he'd have trouble growing grapes up here in Lesswilling but he just shrugged and said cellarvy or something like that.

Anyways, time for a slice of toast and Lurpack. I like a bit of toast with the 10 o'clock news. The wife used to say why don't you throw caution to the wind and try something different like a cracker. Once, she bought this stuff called hummus and tried to get me to taste it but it had garlic in it.

15

She told me I should try to be more adventurous, so the next day, I bought Cross and Blackwell tomato soup instead of Heinz, but she still left me.

It would be easy to feel a bit down right now. No wife, no co-op anymore and the computer still not working properly. Never been the same since he moved in next door. But I try to keep smiling. Like my mother always said, there's always a new bottle to open somewhere. And there were – gin and Lambrusco – hidden under towels, behind the spare blankets, in the laundry basket. One bottle was stashed in the filing cabinet for commemorative stamps in the post office. We found them all after she'd run off with the insurance bloke.

It's never been the same here since he bought next door. First thing he did was redecorate even though there was perfectly good anaglypta on every wall. We'd wallpaper in our dinette that was on when we moved in. Nothing wrong with it, I said, but the wife insisted on painting it Dead Salmon. Said it was appropriate.

Of course, the wife's tickled pink now she has that new place with its open plan this and open plan that and a conservatory full of that wicker furniture. Told me she's bringing the outside in and taking the inside out and breaking down the boundary between home and garden. Well, she'll be bloody cold in winter, that's all I can say, especially in Lesswilling. Told me about some of the colours she'd chosen for their house – Slipper Satin for the main bedroom, Cook's Blue for the kitchen and Lichen in the conservatory. I suggested she tried Sulking Room Pink for the spare room for when her menopause was bad. She said that was the first time I'd made her laugh in 17 years. Then she put the phone down.

Part 4

I said he would. That bloke who moved in next door – he's only had a patio put down near that shed he calls a summer house with a bloody great gas barbecue stuck on it. We don't have barbecues. We have a bonfire in November on the big field and you can buy hotdogs. You get barbecues in Australia, where it's hot and dry, maybe London, but not in Lesswilling. And why in God's name does he need a gas one? I'm not one of them Greenies but there was something in the Daily Mail about how damaging they are to the environment. Mark my words, first the Co-op went; next, it will be the icecap.

Having that patio meant he had to get rid of some perfectly good lawn as well. All it needed was some Weednfeed down and I'd even offered to scarify it for him. He said he never doubted I'd be good at scarifying, but he wasn't into lawns. That doesn't matter, I said. A garden needs a lawn and everybody else in Lesswilling has a lawn. There's been lawns here in every garden since I moved in. He said times change and I was invited to his barbecue anyway. I told him the weather forecast was for rain. He said there were always marquees to hire. That bloke has more money than sense, I reckon. The church had a marquee for their annual fete last year but it collapsed between the prize for best leek and the one for marrows. Just as the vicar's wife was picking up best handtied posy, she disappeared under the tarpaulin and had to be taken to hospital with her angina.

The wife gave me a bit of a shock yesterday. She said she was expecting. Expecting what, I said – a new Farrow and Ball paint chart. She said no, a baby. Now, I might not be a doctor but it seems mighty strange to be expecting a baby after 20 years of hot flushes, bad heads and needing to have her own space. Not a baby baby, she said. Chuck and her had decided to get a puppy. This is the woman who made a fuss if I forgot to change out of my gardening shoes before walking in the house. Now they're having a puppy. A shittypoo or something. Well, I said, you can't say the breed's not a warning, can you? I wouldn't mind but when I suggested we get a goldfish, she point blank refused. Said she'd enough wet fish in her life.

So he's ruined his garden, took up most of his lawn and I noticed last night, he's got fairy lights strung all over, through his acers, up through the holly and some in his damsons. Ostentatious twat. I'm not sure what a twat is but the wife called me it just before she left and I'm guessing it's not a compliment. The dictionary says it's a pregnant fish. She said she'd had enough of wet fish. So I'm putting two and two together and thinking the worst.

Besides, I can't go to his barbecue anyway. I wouldn't want to make this public knowledge of course, but I joined one of those dating site places. Through the paper. I can't get anything on the computer this week but that scene in 2001, Space Oddity – the one where that computer sings Daisy, Daisy. Always thought that were a bit creepy but I didn't really get the film to be honest. I preferred Star Trek; the original series though with Kirk, not when it got daft. Anyway, this dating site. I'm meeting a lady called Phyllis tonight. We spoke a bit on the phone and she says she thinks Farrow and Ball are overpriced and over rated. She likes Crown. I can live with Crown. Excuse me a minute. I've suddenly got Also Sprach Zarathustra coming through the speakers to the computer. I'm not a fan of Strauss and I've no idea why it's playing now. Oh bloody hell, now I'm seeing apes banging bones, and I don't know if it's the same film or the start of Planet of the Apes. It's not Star Trek, I know that. There's no Vulcans.

I think I need the man from Curry's but I'm reluctant to phone. Last time I rang about the tele, he said Bush went out of business some years back and had I considered a Samsung with a 50 inch curved screen and sound surround speakers. I said I only wanted a tele, not a bloody cinema and besides, how do you see round corners. He told me to stop wasting his time and see someone for help. I said I'm asking a Curry's expert here. He said he was having trouble with his reception and he never did phone back.

My mother had a saying for everything. When you could understand her after the gin and lambrusco. She used to say "Yougorrasipafewglassesbeforesyouknowifityerlikesitson". She sipped quite a few glasses before she ran off with the insurance bloke, so dad said. I wonder if Phyllis and I will hit off. I'm taking her for a drink in the Cocks'a' Crowing pub and then for a meal. I looked all over for a Bernie Inn but they went out with Bush, I reckon. So it's the Beefeater in Durham, and bugger the expense. If they do a two for one, even better. Right, I'm off to take the plug out of that bloody computer and then I need to iron a shirt. My sister reckons it's all a bit more casual nowadays eating out. Well, I wouldn't know. Last time was before the wife got the menopause and that was a Bernie Inn. You know where you are with a steak. I'm splashing out on a taxi there and back. There's too many roundabouts for the Micra, and besides I'd like a small glass of House with my steak.

Part 5

What a night! I came home from meeting Phyllis thinking never again; I'd rather have a root canal at the dentist. I knew things had changed since me and the wife were courting. You can see it – a lot more women wear trousers, even in Lesswilling. "Cupid's darts" testimonials from satisfied customers, "Blind dates to fulfil your dreams." Well, meeting Phyllis didn't fulfil my bloody dreams, I can tell you that.

I was a bit taken aback at the cost when I first saw their advert but I thought it had to be worth it to find a loving companion for the twilight years, and it was in the Daily Mail, so I paid the £500 introduction fee, saw the details for Phyllis and rang her. I thought we were so well suited when she said she weren't keen on Farrow and Ball. She preferred Crown. It was music to my ears. I was very optimistic. I was certain we would have so many things in common. I'm not often wrong but I don't mind admitting I was way off the mark there.

I was in the Cock's'a'crowing five minutes early tonight to be on the safe side. I'd toyed with going casual and leaving off the tie but it didn't feel right. I was checking my watch and the door when in she walked. I knew it was Phyllis because she was carrying a copy of a Farrow and Ball paint chart. We both were. It was a little joke we'd agreed to break the ice. I took one look and tried to hide my paint chart down the side of the chair but she was too quick. She spotted me, waved her paint chart in my direction and then there she was in front of me, holding out her hand and I was shaking it and wondering what in God's name I'd done.

She had purple hair. Neon purple. Now, my mother once died her hair, just before she ran off with the insurance bloke but she told us it had been a mistake – the peroxide had been too strong and that's why she was orange. I thought it was maybe because she'd mixed the dye with Lambrusco instead of water but I hadn't liked to say. Mother could be a bit feisty after her lunch. I reckon the gin and Lambrusco didn't hit it off with the brawn butties, but I've no evidence, as they say. Anyways, purple hair. I weren't expecting that. Or the way she was dressed. I like a woman in a frock but a tartan frock over lurex stripy trousers – that was a bit different. I said to myself, Alan, it's Durham, not Lesswilling and maybe she doesn't have a full length mirror at home. And besides I'd paid £500 to meet her. We don't throw good money around up here, not like in London.

I stood up and introduced myself. She asked if I preferred Al but I said no, I preferred Alan. She told me she preferred Phyll to Phyllis and what was I drinking. I suggested I get us a couple of sherries. She said I had a great sense of humour and hers was a large glass of Sauvignon. I was surprised by that, yes, but even more surprised when the bloke just looked at the fiver I held out and laughed. How in God's name can it cost £12.75 for one white wine and a Britvic orange? I thought then if this is modern dating, I can't afford it, so I decided to give Phyllis the benefit of the doubt and hoped for the best.

We started chatting. She told me she was doing an Open University degree in Women's Studies. I said I'd heard of degrees in Media Studies where they watch films, but I'd never realised there were degrees in ironing, cooking and cleaning, and she said I had a wicked sense of humour. Then she asked me what pronoun did I prefer? I admit that threw me a bit, so I pretended to check my shoelace. Then she asked what agenda I most identified with. I wasn't sure what she was on about there. We used to have agendas at the bowling club meetings to start with but no one followed them and we always ended up with Ted Hipkiss arguing with Mrs Hipkiss instead. So I brushed some fluff off my knee, hedged my bets and suggested we get off to eat. That large Sauvignon was nearly gone and I wasn't keen on forking out for another.

She said she didn't fancy the Beefeater and could we go Italian. I thought it was premature to be talking holidays together but I said I'd once thought about Lake Como. She said no, she'd meant going to Pepe's down Gilesgate. I'd never heard of it but she said it was very popular, so I decided to risk it. I had a pizza once from the Co-op and it was ok; not as good as egg and chips but not bad when you added a splash of HP brown sauce, my mother's go-to for adding flavour.

It was a fifteen minute walk to Gilesgate. She was talking about the light on the river and how we could maybe hire a boat one day. I didn't like to admit I get a gippy stomach on water so I just nodded. Time enough, I thought. She said she was 64 this year, but felt like 44 and wanted to experience life in all its wonderful glory after looking after her sick mother for 26 years. I asked if that's when she'd gone purple and she said I was a stute. I decided to look that word up when I got home but it didn't sound like when the wife called me a twat.

I was surprised when she tried linking arms though. You had to be serious before linking when I was courting the wife. She said then she had a very healthy appetite and hoped I did too, so it was good we were there, I said, if she was peckish. I thought it was strange when she patted my arm at that point and made a noise like a growl, but by then I'm thinking, I'm on a date with a woman calling herself a bloke's name who wears frocks over trousers, has no full length mirror, and needs university to learn what women have always done. The evening wasn't what I'd expected but at that point, I was still willing to make the best of it. I'm an easy going sort of bloke in many ways.

So we got sat down at a table by a bloke who was wearing jeans so tight, I could feel my own eyes stinging. He was introduced himself as Luigi, in a strange accent, but I've seen him on a morning serving in Lesswilling post office and he calls himself Kirk there and sounds like me. Then I started looking through the menu for something I could understand and noticed the prices. Hell's teeth. You'd need a mortgage for a steak and a small glass of house red in Pepe's. And there were no two for ones. Or pensioners' specials. I was just thinking, Alan, you're seriously out of your depth here when she tapped my arm, and suggested I might like Fuckoffchia and that's when I knew it was a terrible mistake. "Cupid's darts" wasn't for me. I could take purple hair, a frock over trousers, a bloke's name, but I won't have women swearing. I told her I'd come down with a very bad headache and had to go home. She said she'd get me an Uber but I said, no, I'd get a taxi. That cost me another tenner. This dating thing isn't for me, I was thinking as the taxi pulled up in my street.

Of course, that bloke next door had his barbecue in full swing. He was waving me to go round so I stuck up two fingers like I'd seen them do on Eastenders once. I decided to cancel my subscription straight away. The apes had gone off the computer. Instead, there was a little boy telling a bloke he sees dead people. I don't know which film it was but it doesn't sound very uplifting, does it. I'm sure the same bloke was in Die Hard though. The wife loved that film especially the way his vest got smaller and smaller. I remember saying look, even heroes wear thermals. But she said it wasn't from Damart, was it, and she had a hot flush and could I sleep in the spare bed that night. She'd already made it up for me. I miss her though; she didn't wear strange clothes or have purple hair or call herself a boy's name. But she did run off with Chuck, I reminded myself. I thought right then, bugger it, I'm opening that Cherry Brandy – it had cost me £532.75 already that night and I'd only had a Britivic orange. It didn't really go with the toast and Lurpack but I remembered my mother once saying "Yercan'tcryittillyertriesit". She always rolled her words together after her lunch, did mother.

I was just settling down to look up that word 'stute' when the phone rang. I thought it might be the wife but it wasn't. It was a woman who'd seen my details on "Cupid's darts" and thought we might have things in common. Her name was Crepuscular Rays. She said she reads Tarot cards and likes to engage in communication with the departed. I asked her if that included ex-wives and she said only if they were dead as well as ex. She said lawyers were best for the living sort. Alan, I thought, you've paid your £500 already, so I asked her what she drank. She said she was teetotal. I did the sums and said it would be lovely to meet up. Strange name but at least it's not a bloke's. And a stute isn't another name for a twat, at all. It's German for a female horse. She was a very strange woman, was Phyllis, but I'm hoping that Crepuscular and I might be better suited.

Part 6

So, all I said to the wife was if you want it valuing, you sort it and next thing I know there's an estate agent on the doorstep with a clipboard. I never expected it would come to this. I mean, I know she's been living with Chuck in that new detached in Morewilling for a bit, but I did think that maybe she'd tire of choosing paint colours and having a big fridge freezer. I told her that and she laughed and said she'd been living with a fridge freezer for years. Said being with Chuck had reawakened her passion for life and she wants a divorce. Told me no way was she coming back. They've got plans, her and Chuck. They're turning one of the bedrooms into a walk-in wardrobe and another will be a playroom for the shittypoo. There's a gym in one already. I said she was running out of rooms for her menopause but she said her menopause finished the day she left me. *So much for medical science,* I thought.

She said I could buy her out if I wanted. I told her why would I do that when I'd paid the deposit and the mortgage every month. She said she was legally entitled to half. We didn't have to sell to a stranger. Just an arrangement, with a solicitor. I told her I'd no intention of moving out, she could do her worst and I'd see her in court. I'd heard that in an afternoon tele matinee last week. She said it wasn't like me to be so petulant and childish so I told her to bog off. That's what Kirk in the post office told me to do the other day when I asked why he was calling himself Luigi and talking funny in Pepe's.

Mind, I did tell his grandmother what he'd said to me and she said she'd sort him out; said he was too full of himself by half since he got his City and Guilds. Barbara from Newton Crescent can sort out most folks. Take the binmen. When they didn't take her garden refuse a couple of months ago, she had the rat people down in the hour. I said where did you see the rats then and she just said you don't have to see them, just say you did, and mention your son works in Westminster. I said I thought her son worked in Marks and Spencer's and she said yes, in Westminster Gardens, Milton Keynes, but they didn't need to know that.

Her garden bin was emptied next day. I don't think Kirk has much of a chance, somehow.

Anyway, the estate agent poked around, asked a lot of questions, then said the bungalow would need quite a lot of what he called updating if it were to sell for what it could fetch. I said it had been updated when the previous owners had put in central heating and what else had he in mind. Told me mango bathroom suites with plastic marble taps weren't really in nowadays and maybe think about a bit of a kitchen makeover. I said did he think I had money to burn like next door and he said if I wanted a quick sale, he would strongly recommend it. Well that sorted it. I don't want any sale, let alone a quick one. I told him I'd see what was in the post office savings but I know what's in there already – bugger all, after the subscription to "Cupid's dart". The wife had spent a lot of it already on Farrow and Ball paint before she left. I reckon it was our most of our post office savings that got them that detached in Morewilling. The thing is, I like it here. It's my home. I've lived in Lesswilling all my life and I'm not leaving my herbaceous borders to the mercies of someone like him next door. Someone new might have my buddleia whipped out faster than my auntie Glad's appendix. And she'd only gone in with a sore throat.

I thought before I met up with Crepuscular, I might do a bit of research into her hobby, but I'm no wiser. All I can get on the computer this week is that scene in The Wicker Man where Britt Eckland is banging her bare bottom on a bedroom wall and Edward Woodward is looking uncomfortable. She was once married to Peter Seller, Britt Eckland. For some reason, I had dreams about them for a time. The wife complained about being woken by me banging my bare bottom on the bedroom wall and shouting "you rotten swine, you". Said I sounded just like Bluebottle in the Goons and she'd always hated that character; she'd preferred Neddy Seagoon. I said that was Harry Secombe and Britt weren't married to him. She said I had a knack of sounding very logical even when I was talking crap. I'm not sure if she meant it as compliment or not.

But back to Crepuscular. She's suggested I go to hers for a meal instead of eating in a restaurant. Told me she's a plant eater. I thought that was a strange thing to say but I said I loved vegetables too, especially carrots. She asked how I felt about more exotic vegetables and I said I was fine. I'd had sugar snap peas once when they were on special offer at the Co op. I thought I'd upset her for a minute or two as she went quiet but then she was back on and explaining that there wasn't much she couldn't do with a potato. I said I was relieved to hear it just as she ran out of battery.

I wonder what meat she'll be serving with the vegetables. I'm partial to lamb but I like most meats – if it once lived, I'll eat it. My mother always said if it once had a face, it once had a smile and a smile makes you happy. One day, I did ask her would they still be smiling if the animals had known what was coming. She said have you ever seen a sad turkey in November and if I became one of them that didn't eat meat, I'd be out on my arse faster than she could open the next bottle. I'm going to Crepuscular's tomorrow evening. I have the address on three separate bits of paper and I've put a red line on the Road Atlas to show me the way. I'm leaving nothing to chance. I'll put a flask in the car and a blanket, just in case. I don't think I'll need the snow shovel. Not in August.

Part 7

I'm having a glass of that Cherry Brandy I opened the other night. What in God's name has happened to women? The wife read that book about a female eunuch and told me about the Spice Girls but I wasn't convinced by them. I always preferred The Shangri-las myself. When I was younger, I used to fancy myself as a bit of a leader of the pack, you know. A bit Marlon Brando like. Working in the bank though, you had to be very careful not to upset people. It was either find my wild side or get a mortgage. A mortgage seemed the best way forward, especially if you were living in Lesswilling and I don't regret it. Look what happened to that bloke in the song.

I went to see Crepuscular tonight, like I said I would. I'd set off with an hour to spare so I sat in the car on Asda's carpark when I got there. I was prepared – I'd taken the new Clive Cussler and I had the flask. It's a good job I wasn't any earlier or I might have had to buy something. They only give you one hour free parking in that Asda. But better to be early than to miss the worm, my mother used to say. I'm not sure why. There was one of them security people hovering around but I just held up the flask and smiled. Why do these security guards swagger around when all they've got is a walkie talkie and a pen? My cousin got a job as security in Morrison's a few years back. They were trained not to intervene, not to hurry and not to notice. They could have claimed damages if they'd been hurt tackling someone and the company would have been liable. Apparently, the grannies with scooters were always the most vicious and knew just where to poke their umbrellas. I bet Barbara, Kirk's grandmother, ran training courses for them.

Anyway, I made sure I'd enough tea left in the flask for the way home and made my way to Crepuscular's address at spot on half past. She opened the door and waved so I waved back. She said she was sensing my aura and to stand still, so I explained I'd been sitting in the Asda carpark for a while and maybe I should have opened the window. She said my aura was green, with a purple tinge to its outline and was I musical. I said not really but I liked Evita. Next, I'm being invited inside and shown through to the back of the house. I kept waiting for the right moment to present my Thankyou box of Cadbury's Heroes but she didn't seem to catch breath. She was like a sailboat on steam, as my mother would have said.

She offered me a glass of home-made lemonade and said we were having pak choi on a bed of wild rice. I've never heard anyone pronounce pork chop like that but I thought maybe she was from the south. And the only time I've eaten rice was my mother's rice pudding and I didn't really like that. Probably because she should have cooked it in milk not gin. I asked if there would be any HP to go with it, but she said such things were the food of the devil and I needed a tarot reading before we ate so she could cleanse my chakras. I said I was quite happy to wash my hands but my chakras were out of bounds. I wasn't sure what they were but they sounded private.

So there we were, in her back room and she took out a pack of cards. I was trying to decide how long ago I'd last played cards but my main thought was food. I normally eat with the six o'clock news and Look North would have been nearly finished by now. Crepuscular started dealing out the cards but there was only one hand. I said it would be a bit of a one-sided game and hardly fair, and she told me the cards would offer an insight into my future. I hoped there was a picture of a bloody great plate of food underneath one of them. She told me not to be afraid but to turn over the cards one by one. So I did. Fast. I was desperate to eat and if this had to be endured, fair enough but I decided that next time it would be me who cooked and we would eat with the six o clock news.

The first one had a picture of a magician, upside down. Crepuscular tutted and said if it had been the other way up, it would have meant creativity and originality. I asked what it meant like that and she said a weakness of will and I lacked imagination. I don't know how she could say that with me sitting there in a new paisley tie patiently dying of starvation but I said being upside down was a matter of perspective. It could just as easily be the right way up. Crepuscular just tapped the next card.

It was an image of a tower. She said it symbolised the destruction of old ideas, the smashing of old ways and the opportunity for new erections. I think she said erections but I was beyond listening by that point. I asked if there might be a few chips to go with this roasted pork chop and she said did she look like a woman who'd have a bag of McCains in the freezer. And it wasn't a pork chop. It was pak choi. I said I'd eat packed anything and she told me to pack up and piss off. Said she could never eat with someone whose cards revealed so much anger, futility and despair. I thought that was a bit harsh but I knew I had a Twix in the glove compartment so I just thanked her for a lovely evening and got out fast.

I found out one thing though. She's not not really called Crepuscular Rays. I saw an envelope on the table with her name and address. Her real name is Brenda Smith. I won't be seeing her again, I reckon. So that's two dates now, and with the petrol tonight, it's cost me £542.38 pence and I've had one Britivic Orange and a glass of homemade lemonade out of it all. I'm giving up this dating lark. I might take up bowls again.

Part 8

This morning, I rang Cupid and told her I wanted no more introductions to any ladies looking for a meaningful relationship and she said they had plenty of men as well as those still questioning their gender identity if that were more to my taste. I told her I lived in Lesswilling, not London, and I'd thought Brexit had sorted all that stuff out at the same time as the fishing rights. She said she hoped I find happiness with a loving partner one day and had I considered a dog. She said her spaniel had brought her a great deal of joy and I said I'd always liked spaniels. We agreed they were very affectionate little dogs. So I'm meeting her at the weekend, and the spaniel. I asked if this counted as my third introduction or could I get a refund on my arrangement and she said she'd reimburse me £50. Her name's Fifi. That's the spaniel. I'm not sure about Cupid herself. I would imagine it's not her real name but after my recent experiences, I'm taking nothing for granted. It's not a dinner date this time. Early afternoon seemed a safe bet and it won't cost me anything. She's coming to Lesswilling Park and I said I'd take a flask of tea. She's bringing a bowl and water for Fifi.

Of course, it couldn't last, could it? I like fifteen blueberries with my mid-morning coffee and there were only thirteen left. My mother reckoned that thirteen was unlucky – she said it stemmed from the time she threw up after her thirteenth gin. But like she said, she'd time to practise before her 13th birthday. She didn't give up easily, didn't mother. Until she ran off with the insurance bloke. I can see her now, hankie in one hand, little suitcase in the other, and a bloody great carrier bag stuffed with Lambrusco bottles and a photograph of me in my grammar school uniform wedged between them. The insurance bloke, Ernie, was ducking down from all the stuff dad was throwing at them from the window – dresses, shoes, hats, handbags, corsets all raining down on the path. Ernie put the bag down at one point and raised his fists, shouting "come on then, if you're man enough" but I heard mother tell him she'd no time for male posturing. I'd never heard her use a phrase like that before.

We found a copy of The Feminine Mystique in amongst her emergency bottle supplies a few weeks later and dad said he'd suspected she'd been watching Peyton Place on the quiet too and that programmes like that and Betty Friedan had filled women's heads with notions of self-importance and sexual liberation. He said Ernie would live to regret the day and we would be fine together without her. At 15, it didn't feel like that to me but she moved to France with Ernie a few months later and after a couple of postcards from Dol de Bretagne, I never heard from her again. The last one just said "seize the grapes and squeeze hard, Alan." She was a bit of a poet, was Mother.

But getting back to this morning. I'd just finished the last blueberry when the post arrived. I do prefer it to arrive just before my coffee break but Stan is getting on a bit now and that brute down at number ten always has a go at his ankles.

It's a Jack Russell, not a Spaniel. So, I skimmed through the prepaid funeral plan, put the bowel cancer screening kit to one side with all the others and then looked at the last one. It was a letter from a solicitor. Octopus Fields was acting on my wife's instructions. He informed me and basically I needed to get a solicitor of my own because she wanted a divorce and he was hereby serving me with the necessary papers for a no fault divorce, as allowed under British law from April 2022. Octopus Fields could go and take a running jump, I thought. If there were no fault, there was no reason for a divorce, and she'd come round eventually. But I read on anyway. Octopus Fields went on to say my wife had thought I might be a little unwilling so he was also including the necessary papers for a divorce based on my unreasonable behaviour. It was up to me as to which I preferred but he did strongly advise seeking legal representation. He finished by saying he was acutely aware of the distress this might cause and hoped I'd have a nice day.

Unreasonable behaviour, I thought. I don't think so. While I was pondering what I'd ever done that might be considered unreasonable, the phone rang and it was the wife. She said Chuck had suggested Octopus Fields rather than Smudgit and Fudgit from the High Street. Octopus Fields was an experienced divorce lawyer who got the best for the client. She was sorry but her and Chuck felt a clean break was necessary, but she would be quite happy with a no fault, no quibble quickie and half the estate. I said I thought there'd been enough quickies at her end recently and I'd found the mark on the wall in the dining room and had the Dead Salmon paint come off in the shower.

I then explained that the neighbours wouldn't agree to her having half the estate. They might do that sort of thing in the

States but not here in Lesswilling, where every man's home is his castle. She said the estate was what we owned – the bungalow and the savings. I told her the savings had gone on one woman called Phyll and one called Crepuscular, who'd turned out to be a Brenda. She said she had always been a bit worried about my mental health and perhaps I should get some help. I told her I was perfectly fine, I was seeing a spaniel called Fifi at the weekend and that's when she put the phone down.

I tried looking up Octopus Fields on the computer but it was playing up yet again. Steve McQueen on the bike in The Great Escape, ending up in the barbed wire but some clever bugger had set it to Singing in the Rain. Over and over again. I just don't know what's happened to that bloody computer. I blame it on him next door. Come to think of it, I've not seen him for over a week. And there's been no clinking to his recycling bin. Either he's gone away for a break, or he's absconded on his mortgage or he's dead. With a bit of luck, it will be one of the last two.

Part 9

He's back. Heard the taxi pulling up at some unGodly hour last night – well after News at Ten. Then it's clink, clink, clink, up the path, then squeaking wheels from a suitcase, and him shouting "hey up, Alan, stop hiding behind that curtain and have a drink to welcome me back." So I thought, right, I've had enough of his provocation and taunts. It's time for this worm to turn. So I changed out of my slippers, put on my shoes and tie, went outside and rang his bell. You should have seen his face when he saw my face. He said this was a real surprise but to go round the back and he'd open up the summer house.

It's got electric. I wouldn't like his next fuel bill, I tell you. I'd not been that close to his shed before so I did feel a bit awkward standing there on the patio next to the gas barbecue after all I'd said but the moment passed when I stood on the snail and heard it crunch. *Splat,* I thought. *That's one little patio stain he weren't expecting.* I was looking around for a few more to splat when out he came, carrying a tray. He said it was just a few nibbles, he'd not eaten since arriving back in England and what was I drinking. I replied a nice cup of decaffeinated tea would hit the spot and he laughed. Said he didn't do tea. He could do coffee, strong, black, or would that upset my circadian rhythms. I hadn't anticipated there'd be dancing so I said a small glass of water would be acceptable.

He said he had a complete bar in the summer house but it didn't include water. I could have beer, wine, vodka, gin, whisky; said he had a particularly fine malt and a very smooth cognac. I asked if he had any mixers and he reeled them off too… So I said I'd have a slimline tonic. He said he knew when he was beaten and would I like a few nibbles from the tray. I looked at all the little bowls and tried to work out which were the crisps. He's pointing to them and telling me – something called Cornyshuns, like gherkins you can buy in The Pride of Plaice to go with chips but tiny. Some funny strips of something he called fried loumi. I bet they were insects. There was a bowl of pink stuff; he did say the name but it looked like the ointment mother had once put on my Chicken Pox to stop me scratching, so I didn't risk that. I asked if there were any crisps and he got out some Pringles. I only normally touch Walker's but I showed willing and took a couple.

He said he'd been away on holiday and was I planning a break. I was just about to answer him when I realised that I was sleeping with the enemy, so to speak. The wife had rented that a few years ago and insisted I watch it with her. We never finished watching it though. I just couldn't see that woman's problem – I like tins facing the right way too. Who doesn't? And there's no reason in God's earth why someone can't hang up a towel correctly. The wife sided with the woman of course and took the film back to Blockbusters the next day. But now, I was sitting with a man who had wrecked a Lesswilling lawn, erected an eyesore and whose recycling bins must have more empty bottles than the local pub.

I told him thanks for the drink, but I'd had a very stressful day with Octopus Fields and needed to get some sleep. He asked if Octopus Fields was a person or a cephalopod so I said neither. He was a lawyer. Then I went home. I decided that being impetuous was a dangerous path to take and to be a bit more controlled in the future. A moment of weakness and your knickers are round your ankles, my mother used to say. And dad said she should have known.

Today was dust and vac day. I find a routine very soothing, so when the wife left, I got one of those Week at a Glance calendars and went through each day; washing and ironing Mondays, dust and vac Tuesdays, Wednesdays clean windows, Thursdays rotate the tins in the cupboard and check for expiries, and Fridays are shopping. It looked very full by the time I got to December. I have a separate one for the garden because that's seasonal. You don't deadhead your roses in the middle of winter, do you? The wife used to say I was on the artistic spectrum, and I suppose gardening can be creative. If you know what you're doing and don't plant an herbaceous in the middle of a bloody lawn, like he did next door.

Anyway, there I was – dusting done, I switched on the vac, pop and then nothing. Checked the fuse. Shook it a bit. Nothing. Found the guarantee in my little file box but that had run out in 1998. Alan, I said, you need a new vac. Well, it was no use looking on the computer because Steve McQueen was still singing in the rain so it was a trip to Curry's. Why in God's name do they make it so difficult to find a new vac? There were rows and rows of the buggers. I asked one of the assistants if he could help.

He asked me what make I fancied. I said I'd always been very happy with my Electrolux. He could better that, he said, and they had a good deal on a robotic. I explained I wanted a vacuum not something from Terminator. He asked if I'd consider an Animal. I said no, the wife was getting a shittypoo but right now my priority was getting a new vac. He said they had an amazing deal on a Dyson V15 detect absolute. It was cordless, powerful, intelligent… I stopped him there. It's a vacuum cleaner, I said, not a member of Mensa. Actually, I always wanted to be a member of Mensa but they said my IQ fell a bit short. 32 points short, and I struggled with the shapes. And the numbers. I wasn't too hot on the words either but I made a good stab at those.

Anyway, this Curry's man said the V15 was a great deal at £629.99. £629.99, I said; I lived in Lesswilling not up the hill like the wife. He said they were very popular so I said that might be so but I'd spent the last of my savings on an introduction agency and I'd only had a Britivic orange and a homemade lemonade to show for it. He said he could introduce me to some very willing ladies and he only worked in Curry's part time. He gave me his card and told me to ring any time. I put it in my pocket and asked what vacs they had for under £50. He said try the reconditioned place down the high street. I'm getting very disillusioned by Curry's so I thought I'd try it. They had a reconditioned Beko for £54.95. Bit pricy but dust and vac successfully achieved for today by the Six o'clock news. Windows tomorrow.

I'm just looking at the card Curry's Man gave me. "Buxom Beauties to do your bidding". I put it in the drawer with the bowel cancer screening stuff.

Part 10

So I've managed to get to the end of the week's schedule without further domestic challenge. Tins rotated yesterday, expiries sorted out – just the one jar of preserved lemons this week, from the wife's dalliance with Rick Stein's Mediterranean Odyssey. I think she dallied with Jamie Oliver shortly after that but then Farrow and Ball and the American replaced any cookery inclinations altogether.

When she first left, rotating tins and expiries took nearly all day. There was stuff in the cupboards I'd never heard of. I mean, who in Lesswilling eats artichoke tips? And what are you meant to do with a sundried tomato? They looked like the things that used to crawl up the wall in the back room of the post office. I'm not one to waste food but they went out whether they'd passed their sell-by date or not. "You've expired here", I told them. I didn't even think they'd be welcome in the food bank trolley in the supermarket. Not unless you could chop them into a tin of baked beans and serve on toast. But I admit my understanding of fine cuisine is limited to Masterchef and nowadays, you can't get on that unless you can already open a scallop without losing a finger and do something fancy with a blob of cream and one spoon.

I tried volunteering in the local food bank, the one in the church hall on Misgivings Street. I was quite enjoying it but I wasn't too keen on how they just put things in carrier bags with no system. I made a few constructive suggestions. They told me it would take too long to place them in alphabetical order and there was no way we could organise them into suggested meal planners. When they tried me on distribution instead of packing, they didn't like the way I was asking people how many meals they could make for a family of four with one bag of potatoes and a sliced white. So we decided to part ways. I was only there a day so it wasn't a wrench.

That Octopus Fields rang this morning. Well, his secretary did. Had I managed to consider the letter sent earlier that week. Yes, I had. Was I able to tell them which of the two options I was considering. Neither. She strongly advised me to seek a solicitor's opinion as soon as possible. I told her I was a man who made up his own mind, thankyou very much and I didn't need some Octopus telling me what I could and couldn't do. She said my wife had warned I might say this. I told her my wife's bottom was imprinted in Dead Salmon on the dining room wall now and forever more so she was hardly a credible character witness. That shut her up so I put down the phone. Terminated, I thought.

I got to the supermarket just five minutes later than I normally would so that was a relief. What wasn't a relief was the lack of fresh bread on the shelves by 9.55 and then I was accosted by some woman who told me I wasn't being fair to other customers. I said I was perfectly entitled to check the freshness of the sliced white before purchasing and if that meant squeezing every one of them, I would. And I had. Besides, I told her, I was going back to one I'd picked out originally so she could have her pick. She didn't even want sliced white. She threw a Hovis in her trolley and stormed off. I met her again at the cheese counter not ten minutes later, coming in the opposite direction. She asked if I was stalking her and I said the only thing I was stalking was a nice piece of mature. She said I was the most ignorant man she'd ever met and I told her she should get out more. She went off to find the manager and I decided I could manage without more baked beans this week; I'd already got 14 at the last count yesterday. Then came the paying bit. Why in God's name do they now expect you to stand and scan your own stuff? There was a time when a shopkeeper looked after the customer. Now, they just stand around with a big cardboard arrow and tell you which till you can use. By the time I'd pressed for assistance four times, finished paying, and checked the itemised receipt, I had seconds to clear the store before that woman. I waved at her though as I left, and she stuck up two fingers. I wondered if she was related to Phyll but I wasn't going to ask.

I tried the computer again a few minutes ago. I wanted to look up the history of the east coast railway. Steve Mc Queen's not singing in the rain on his motorbike anymore though. It's the bit in "It's a wonderful life" where George Bailey is on the bridge and then Clarence jumps in and George goes to save him. Only someone's played about with it and all you can hear is Joseph's voice shouting "two more for down below" and manic laughter. It's not like the scene you get at Christmas at all. I should know – I've watched it every year for the past fifty four. That and the Goode Life Christmas special since 1977. Not sure if I can face them this Christmas. Not thinking about the wife and Chuck stuffing a turkey together. I think I can safely indulge in a small Cherry Brandy tonight though. It's Friday. Some people go out on a Friday night, the wife once told me. Looking back, maybe she was dropping a hint. Hindsight's a wonderful thing, my mother used to say; you meet your own arse coming back.

Part 11

I don't mind admitting that I wasn't really looking forward to today when I got up. Making arrangements to meet a woman I've never met and a spaniel in the park was very out of character for me. I reckoned that new neighbour had upset my circadian after all. I'd looked up the word when I got back that night by the way, and it's nothing to do with dancing. I think him and his shed, and his herbaceous island on top of the co-op closing down has all had a bit of an impact. That and the wife leaving. When I think about it, I was quite reckless getting that new vac the other day without going near a copy of Which magazine. I'm normally quite a cautious man and like to do the research first; the wife said cautious wasn't the way she'd phrase it – anally retentive was more accurate.

On the other hand, I'd learned a few new words recently – twat, stute and circadian. And how to pronounce pork chop like they do in London, pak choi. I now knew an upside down magician wasn't a good Tarot card if you wanted to impress the ladies and that modern dating in a pub wasn't something you did if you wanted change from a fiver. I'd also discovered a glass of Cherry Brandy went down a treat with toast and Lurpack. And I had no bloody artichoke tips or preserved lemons clogging up my shelves. My tins were all facing the right way and my towels were hanging straight. Alan, I said over breakfast, life is different but seize the grapes and squeeze, like your mother told you.

So at 2.45 this afternoon, I was standing in the park looking for a woman called Cupid and a spaniel called Fifi. I wondered if Cupid would be wearing a frock over trousers like Phyll or a turban like Crepuscular. Or even if she'd turn up. I'd brought the flask as promised just in case. I'd been there for a good ten minutes and was just about to walk off when this voice asked was I Alan. I'd seen this lady a few minutes before but she looked normal. Then I noticed the spaniel. I said you must be Fifi and she said no, the spaniel was Fifi but she was Rose. She was wearing a skirt, she didn't have purple hair, and she looked like someone I might talk to in the butcher's. Things were looking up.

We started walking around the park. She even let me hold the dog's lead for a bit at one point and Fifi seemed quite settled when we stopped at a bench and had an ice cream. Not Fifi; Rose said giving a dog human food wasn't fair to the animal which I agreed was responsible, although I know nothing about the canine diet. She told me her business was Cupid's Dart but that wasn't her name, and she'd set it up after her husband had died a few years ago. Just for something to occupy her time really. I told her about my ex-wife and the Farrow and Ball man and she said she knew what loneliness felt like. I told her about my system for the household chores and she said she had a similar system herself but it was on a spreadsheet on her laptop. I admitted I wasn't that up-to-date with technology and about the problems with my computer. She said she had a degree in IT and could perhaps come over

48

one afternoon and have a look to see if she could sort it. She seemed very nice for a woman with a degree.

It was five o clock before I knew it. We'd finished the flask so I suggested we stop for a pot of tea and cream scones at The Rainbow's End tea rooms but of course they were closing. Rose said perhaps we could do that another day and that she had really enjoyed herself. And so had Fifi. Well, I said, that makes three of us and I'd never enjoyed a walk quite so much. So we agreed I would ring her and we would arrange to meet again. I gave Fifi a bit of a head tickle, shook hands with Rose and went off home with a bit of a spring in my step. This going for a walk lark had been a real cheap alternative to a date and with the £50 rebate from Cupid's Darts, I was back in pocket, give or take the original £500.

I was in such a good mood when I got back home. I didn't even notice the neighbour was having a barbecue party. Until the smoke wafted over my fence. I was out there in a flash to tell him to keep it on his side. It was my legal right not to have to put up with overhangs from his garden and what would have happened if my washing had been on the line. Cleverclogs said he avoided Mondays for that reason. I asked if he'd been snooping around my calendar to know that and he said everyone in Lesswilling knew about my Mondays, Wednesdays and Fridays. I told him he didn't know everyone in Lesswilling for one thing and for another, if he didn't stop his smoke drifting over my herbaceous, I was calling the police.

Well, he didn't so I did and 999 told me to stop wasting the time of the emergency services or I would be prosecuted. I said I paid my rates and taxes, unlike some, and was entitled to a better customer service. 999 told me to go forth and multiply and rang off. Between them and the Curry's experts, there's not much to choose anymore, is there?

Part 12

I knew the neighbour would be having a lie in after last night's party so I decided to break with tradition and mow the lawn Sunday morning. I even put the new vac on in the bedroom first. Just left it running for a bit to make sure he was awake. And I turned up the radio and had Ride of the Valeries going full pelt too. Even I had a headache after that. I never knew that was written by that Wagner bloke, but you learn something new every day, if you keep an open mind. He was the one who played Napoleon Solo in Man from Uncle. It all had the desired effect – he was shouting over the fence at half past seven this morning. I told him I had as much control over my sounds as he had over his barbecue smoke and to bugger off.

The wife rang just as I was having my blueberries. Asked what was I playing at. She felt Octopus had been very fair in giving me options, and why had I told her about the stain on the wall. I said if she minded others knowing, she should have avoided wet paint. Besides I'd only told his secretary. She said Octopus had rung me herself and was a woman. Well, that was a bit of a surprise. It's not a very feminine name is it, I said. I told her about Cupid being Rose and said names seemed to be a bit misleading nowadays. She said she didn't give a flying fig about names and to sign the bloody papers. So I told her to make me an offer I couldn't refuse and I might consider it. She muttered something about horses and heads and slammed down the phone.

As I washed the car, I wondered if Rose and Fifi might like a little spin out. It needn't be miles, I said, when I rang her. Rose said what she would really like was that pot of tea and cream scones and a little walk around the park again for Fifi. I did the sums – no petrol, no parking, tea and scones …… seemed a reasonable deal, especially as she insisted on paying half. So we agreed I would meet her at the same place in the park and she would book a table at the tea shop for 2:30 pm.

I must say that after living with the wife's menopause for over 30 years, I do find Rose very easy company. We have quite a lot in common. She likes Lurpack on toast and thinks a small sherry before a meal very adequate. I told her about the large Sauvignon incident and she said she was going to include a new screening question about what clients like to drink when they signed up for Cupid's Darts. She said there was a clearly huge difference between a small sherry personality and a large Sauvignon and she'd replace the question on what you'd rescue first if your house were on fire. This time, when we shook hands, she gave mine a little squeeze. I might take her some flowers next time. From the garden, that is. Who in God's earth pays over a fiver for one hydrangea but that's what they charge in that Seeds R Us. I rang the council over that name when it opened. Said we didn't need poor spellings in Lesswilling but they said they'd no department for crimes against the English language and put me through to Refuse.

The neighbour was in his garden again when I got back. Another bloody barbecue and I'm sure he was wafting the smoke over my way. I told him if my buddleia started wilting, I'd squirt his barbecue with the hose pipe. He said the wife had told him my buddleia had wilted years ago and that's why she'd left me. I don't really know if I prefer the word twat or stute in a situation like that. They both sound good out loud. I chose "stute" and said it with as much venom as I could muster. That shut him up.

So, I was just settling down to that new quiz show, "I'm a nonentity, get me out of here", when I heard the postbox. *Hey up,* I thought, *that can't be Stan the postman, not on a Sunday; he's not that slow.* There was a card lying on the mat. It said "From an admirer. Look outside." Now, I'm not normally a suspicious sort of person but I did wonder just who in God's earth would leave me a bunch of flowers on the doorstep, and on a Sunday evening?

There could be only one person, I decided, so I put on my shoes and tie again and went next door. He was still there with his cronies. I asked him what he was playing at. He said he'd no idea why I was taking him flowers but he'd find a vase. That took me back a bit. I asked if it had been him who left them, and he said why would he want to do that. One of them said he'd seen a woman drive up, carry them up my path and then drive off. Did she have a spaniel, I asked. No, she had dark glasses and a sun visor. Well, I don't know any woman who has a sun visor, I told him. You do now, said the crony and looks like she's a bit smitten from the size of her blooms. I told him not to be so crude and left them singing a song about Barnacle Bill the sailor.

What do you do with a bunch of flowers? I thought. I didn't remember seeing a vase but then I never went in the wife's side of the Plan sideboard. So I had a rummage in there and found one that was from Tenerife. We'd never been to Tenerife and I started wondering just what she had got up to when I was on one of those bank training courses I'd never applied for but which I got sent to every year by the area manager. I'd thought I was being groomed for an executive position, until they replaced me with an ATM on the wall outside. I remember the very last one I went on; CRAP – Customer Relations and Partnerships. They put us up in a hotel in Hartlepool and that was crap too.

I'd missed the new quiz programme me by this time of course so I decided to have a look on Google to see how much a Flying Scotsman would cost me nowadays. No success – Jimmy Stewart had gone but all I could get was Sean Connery playing an Egyptian with a Scottish accent in a film about a Highlander. I'm not sure it would convince me to go to Scotland – the views were quite impressive but I'm not sure where the swords came in. That's the trouble with adverts nowadays; they all think they they're up for an Oscar and try to be clever. It was the closest I got to a Scotsman tonight though and I wondered if I should ask Rose to take a look at the computer after all. You'd never think she has a degree – she says pork chop just like I do.

So, I thought I would listen to the radio until toast and Lurpack time, but it was Haven't a Clue. The wife used to say that to me all the time in the last few weeks before she ran off to live with the American. I'd say something like should we plant red geraniums next to the purple begonias and she'd roll her eyes and say 'You haven't a clue, Alan, have you?' I

wouldn't mind but I was only asking out of politeness –
everyone knows they'd clash.

Part 13

Breakfast today went without drama, which is quite normal nowadays. You can't really go wrong with two Weetabix and a pot of tea. The wife had porridge oats for years and stuck most to the pan, but when she discovered Farrow and Ball, she developed a taste for green sludge, in something called a blender which always left a puddle. When she went, so did the blender – in the bin with all sorts of other electrical appliances I found hidden in cupboards. Who in God's earth needs an electric soup maker when you can buy Heinz? And try as I might, there was no way I could get that thing called a Rabbit to open a tin. It didn't do screw lids either. I did ask her at the time why she'd bought a bread maker and she said it was to remind her that some things do still rise. Still ended up in the cupboard though.

She could be ruthless with a fused plug, the wife, despite knowing about my special tin filled with amps, fuse wire and my favourite screwdriver for plugs. She once threatened to mix up the contents of all my tins just so she could see the look of utter panic on my face. I was sure she was joking then but I'm not so sure now. I was telling Rose about my tins and she said that her Gerald had been a very methodical man too.

I like that word, methodical. It's better than an anally retentive git.

Washing and ironing day, I have my routine – fill the twin tub, put it on, go out to set up the rotary line in the garden, and when I get back inside, it's time to rinse in the spinner. I don't mind having to wring out them by hand. Like my mother always said, if there's life left in one side, they don't need burying yet. She'd said that about auntie Mabel when she'd had a stroke and uncle Fred never spoke to her again afterwards. He said mother was insensitive and she was off their Christmas card list for ever but mother just shrugged and said she hated the bloody things; they were dust gatherers from people who just wanted one back to feel popular, and she always shoved them in a drawer until the 2nd January when they went in the bin along with the boxed hankies.

She didn't really do Christmas, didn't mother, other than a dried up turkey she started cooking on Christmas Eve and enough alcohol to get her through till the shops opened again. She made a mean gin trifle though and the sprouts were always flamed in brandy although I think that was a mix up before it became a family tradition. I reckon she just got the sprouts and the pudding confused one year and didn't like to say. When she ran off with Ernie, dad killed off that tradition and we had carrots instead, the gin trifle became strawberry Angel Delight and we had stuffing on the same plate as the turkey instead of Christmas pudding. In some ways, it was more like other people's dinners from then on but I did miss the excitement of not knowing quite what would appear on your plate each Christmas Day. I missed seeing the fire brigade too; the first time, they came to put out the pudding fire. The year after, it was the sprouts. They brought us a fire blanket that time and told mother to be less enthusiastic with the brandy. And the whisky. And possibly the gin too. It got to the stage we would put out a mince pie and a sherry for them on Christmas morning.

Trouble today was when I got back inside to start rinsing and wringing, the first part of the washing was still sitting waiting to happen. I couldn't believe it – after 40 odd years. I would have liked to have marked its passing but when most of your clothes are still dirty but soaked, you need to act fast. I thought, *right, Curry's Expert, you have a chance to redeem yourself.* I rang them up and asked what twin tubs they had in stock. Clearly not an expert really because he asked what was a twin tub so I was explaining when he suddenly asked was this some kind of joke. Turns out they don't make twin tubs anymore, just automatics which have to be plumbed in. By the time he'd finished, I'd done the sums and worked out it was going to be cheaper to go to Linda's Laundrette off High Street. At least until I'd got enough in the savings again.

So there I was in Linda's Laundrette when by rights I should have been pruning the buddleia and edging the lawn with the scissors, when I heard "Well, if it's not the cheesy stalker". It was that bloody woman from the supermarket last week. I decided silence was the best response but she wasn't having it. There were three others in there and she was telling them how I stalked her earlier in the week and how a woman wasn't safe around a cheese counter anymore. I wasn't having that. I said I'd been looking for a tasty piece of cheddar not a dried up old prune and that women like her would always be safe, wherever they happened to be. Old Mrs Prentiss who dishes out the soap powder piped up and said rape was a crime of power not sex, and she'd read that in Spare Rib years ago.

I asked what spare ribs and butchers had to do with it and before you knew it, there was a scuffle and a laundry basket went through the air. That's when Linda came out of her office and it went very quiet.

She told us we were more trouble than the university students. At least they sat and read quietly and didn't argue or throw laundry baskets at each other. I was about to remonstrate and say only one basket had been thrown but she held up one finger and shook her head. Threatened to bar the lot of us if we didn't behave. You're not in a strong bargaining position when your Y Fronts are floating in a dryer along with your shirts and socks, so I sat back down with my Clive Cussler. Mrs Prentiss went back to weighing her soap powder out and the others packed away and left.

Suddenly, I see a cup of tea beside me and do I take sugar. That woman again. She says she might have been a bit hasty the other day and she always took a flask to the launderette and if I'd accept, it might serve as an apology. I said there was no apology needed, I didn't take sugar and I'd been a little vexed the other day too. She said she'd just moved into Lesswilling, was feeling a bit lonely and didn't make friends easily. I said I knew the feeling and that a nice walk in the park might make her feel better.

So, the upshot is we are meeting the day after tomorrow at the park. She's called Barbara, like Kirk's grandmother, and hates it being shortened. I've decided I like the park. It costs me nothing in petrol and you can take a flask. And I think we will have things to talk about too because her last words today were "Just think, if it hadn't been for a delay at Curry's end, I'd never have been in here today." I said I'd a few stories about that lot as well. So that's Rose tomorrow afternoon and Barbara on Wednesday. I will need to jiggle a few of the afternoon chores around but Barbara said flexibility and adaptability have ensured mankind's survival so I reckon I will be safe if the herbaceous only gets a quick forking over this week.

Part 14

Would you believe it, him from next door arrived just as I was about to pour my morning tea this morning. He said the neighbours had all been very worried when the rotary line had come out yesterday but the washing hadn't followed; so worried they'd drawn straws to see who would come round to check I wasn't lying dead in a chair. I assured him that when I died, it would be with dignity in my bed, not slumped in a chair. He said you didn't get to decide when the grim reaper paid a call, then he stopped and said on second thoughts, maybe the grim reaper would make an exception in my case. I said the grim reaper would probably have the decency not to call before I'd poured my morning cupper, which was going to be much stronger than I like it. Two teabags, a three minute wait in the pot, then pour. I know how I like my tea and I dare say the grim reaper does too.

I explained it was my twin tub, and after I'd explained what a twin tub was, he said I could pop round to use his machine any time I liked. I was just about to refuse on principle but did the sums quickly. Once a banker, always a banker. Mother had a similar saying but it started with a different letter. I asked if he would charge me for electricity and when he said no, it was just an neighbourly thing to do, I said I'd bring my own Persil and see him next Monday at 10 am. He said it would be nice to get to know each other a bit better. I didn't like to tell him that whilst I was willing to compromise my principles for the sake of free clean Y Fronts, there was no way I could be friends with a lawn hater, so I just nodded like the wife used to when she couldn't be bothered arguing. Not that I'd realised that at the time. I just thought the power of my reasoning had convinced her. Finding the imprint of her bottom on our wall had made me question a great many things since and then that vase from Tenerife had been the final nail in the coffin of marital trust.

Speaking of which, those flowers were still going strong in the corner. I was wondering again who would send me flowers when the phone rang. It wasn't ten yet and this was the second unexpected event of the day. I hoped to God it wasn't an omen of another appliance breaking down but no, it was Octopus Fields. She asked me if I had made a decision yet and I told her that when I did, she'd be first to know but until I did, she should assume no news was no news. I heard what sounded like a laugh then she said she had been talking with her client, my wife, and another option was now on the table for me to consider and it would be in my interests to hear what she had to say.

It turned out that the imprint of my wife's bottom on the dining room wall was evidence of her infidelity and a clear sign of her being in flagrante. I told her that I had proof of her being in Tenerife too but she said Flagrante was enough. I need to consult the atlas for that one later; it sounds like Italy. Mizz – not Mrs or Miss – Fields had felt bound to advise her client of my right to challenge the divorce on such grounds since many judges took against a philandering wife and found in favour of the cuckoo's husband. She said that the new offer was a quick, uncontested divorce but that the wife would have to buy me out for half the value of the property as established by taking an average of three quotes by three different local estate agents. I would keep all the furniture.

I suggested it was a bit unusual for a solicitor to be advising things in my favours, rather than her client's but she said the law was the law and besides she didn't like unfairness. She asked how long I would need to make a decision because she could get the ball rolling fairly rapidly and it could be in writing with a signed affidavit before noon if I agreed. She also mentioned she'd looked into current house values in Lesswilling and that even with the coloured bathroom suite, I was looking confidently at over £200,000. I said the quicker my balls rolled, the happier I'd be. She said to leave it with her, greased balls rolled very quickly and Chuck was happy to grease as freely as needed to ensure life in Morewilling was as free from embarrassment as possible. Then she said she hoped I liked the flowers she'd left.

Now, I'm not a man normally stuck for words but that did throw me. A woman buying a man flowers is a new one on me. Sometimes, the wife organised flowers for winners' wives at the bowls club but who in God's earth heard of men being given flowers. She was explaining that she'd found the card that should have been with them just the day before on the back seat of her car. I asked if she had a sun visor and she said yes, she had a few, but to get back to the message on the missing card, would I care to have lunch with her one day. Her treat of course. Now, I'm not averse to this Women's Liberation stuff but I draw the line at a woman paying for a man's meal. Then again, I thought – I was saving for a new washing machine and she might drink Sauvignon. I told her I would love to have lunch with her as long as it wasn't at Luigi's on Gilesgate. She said Luigi's was overrated and pretentious and suggested she bring a picnic for us to take to the park. I had to box clever with the day of course, given other commitments, so suggested Thursday to avoid a clash with Rose and Barbara. Not that I mentioned them of course. After all, Octopus would be greasing my balls and I didn't want to upset her before the house was signed firmly in my name.

I did mention Octopus and Barbara to Rose later. It didn't seem right not to. Rose said it was perfectly understandable that a man with my electric tastes would attract the attention of very different ladies. I told her I'd never seen myself as electric and the wife had once said she'd seen more energy in a graveyard. Rose said my wife had clearly been a woman of limited vision but that she had said eclectic, not electric. I thought, I must look it up later to see what it means and then add it to my growing list of new words I'm keeping but a flourish of the tea flask, a Tupperware of ginger nuts and a treat for Fifi proved a successful diversion to cover any embarrassment at the time.

I looked up eclectic earlier over a small Cherry Brandy, by the way. I don't think I'm any the wiser really but it's a step up from boring old fart. Another term of endearment from the wife before she left.

Part 15

Today began well. Windows cleaned without incident, enough blueberries for morning coffee and a very pleasant walk and chat with Barbara this afternoon. She's a keen gardener like myself and we agreed that island beds in the middle of a lawn are a horticultural abomination. She said men like him next door had too much time, too much money and not enough sense; a pellock, in other words. She thought Alan Titsmarsh had been a pellock too on Gardeners' World although she loved Monty Don. I suggested neither of them could really match Percy Thrower plant for plant and Barbara said perhaps not, but at least Monty had two cute dogs. She thought some of the ideas were a bit OTT though like those tubs. I didn't like to tell her it was spelt HOT but I realized it had been a premonition when I got home. There was one of them in next door's garden and I could see it clearly from my back door.

I went round to tell him it was a violation of my human rights to keep coming back to find yet more unwanted changes. He said the changes were in his garden, not mine and that hot tubs were the new must have so I told him straight – not in Lesswilling they weren't. Baths were private events to be enjoyed in your home behind frosted glass and a lock –

always would be, always had been. Not strictly true, I admit. Mother once put the tin bath in the back yard, took off all her clothes and charged the neighbours a shilling to come and have a look. She said it was her version of Bob a Job. Father put a stop to it when he came home of course. Old Mr Turner never forgave him for that. He'd been raiding his stash of coins for the gas meter all afternoon and hadn't budged. He said the memory of my mother would warm him up when the gas meter ran out.

But there's a big difference between a tin bath for one and a hot tub for six, I reckon. And where's the pleasure sitting half naked in a bath in the garden when the nights are drawing in and there's a real nip in the air. It can't be good for your extremities. He said people thought them fun and maybe I remembered what fun was from the distant past. I said I had quite enough fun in my life now, thank you very much, without going all wrinkly holding a cheap glass of plonk and a Pringle. I told him I was going to report him to the council for having unplanned erections in his garden and when he laughed, I stuck up one finger, like Barbara had showed me, and came back home to ring the council. I didn't get very far. I'd only given my name and address and they asked if it was another complaint about crimes against the English language. When I said no, it was about unplanned erections, the bloke said I should think myself lucky, he had to use Viagra, but he'd put me through to refuse anyway. I don't think they have any other departments in that bloody council.

After all that kerfuffle, I was nearly ten minutes late having my tea and the final straw was finding out I'd run out of brown sauce; egg and chips with no HP. Another travesty. I couldn't understand how it had happened. I keep a list of "running lows", another list for "almost outs" and then I transfer any empties to the shopping list Thursday evening. I could only think I'd had so much going on with Rose and Barbara, household appliance malfunctions and that bloody neighbour, that I must have missed the brown sauce. I must make sure I double check both lists tomorrow when I do my rotations. I wouldn't want my systems collapsing at this stage, not when they were working like a well-oiled machine. Mother told me she was well-oiled once but I think that was to explain why she'd put an Airmail stamp on a parcel to Southampton. The customer was a bit surprised when she tried to charge him for postage to South Africa. Mother apologized and said she'd thought it said Cleethorpes. I'm not sure whether that wasn't worse but the customer went off quite happy.

I tried again tonight to find how much it would cost to replace my Flying Scotsman but Google had other ideas. I couldn't tell you what film it was but it had a lot of naked nuns throwing themselves on Oliver Reed and doing things with candles. Not my cup of tea at all. But then, I was brought up a Methodist and they manage without nuns. They're not keen on alcohol, or gambling either so it was always a mystery to me why Mother married my father in the first place. She was partial to a flutter on the horses as well as a drink. She used to say if alcohol was so bad, why did Jesus work his miracles on water at parties, and she bet it was why he was invited in the first place because he didn't sound a bundle of laughs the rest of the time. She once stuck a picture of a bottle of Guinness over the lantern on a print of William Holman Hunt's Light of the World. Father said she'd burn in hell for that and she said it was better to burn out than to fade away.

In the end, I just listened to a play on radio 4 until toast and Lurpack time. I couldn't tell you what it was called but some chap called Godot never turned up. It all seemed a lot of fuss about nothing to me. I lost interest so I don't know if he ever did get there. I just hope that it wasn't a premonition for tomorrow as I'm curious to meet this Octopus woman. She rang just after I'd finished washing up tonight – said she wanted to check if I had any allergies or intolerances. I told her I was a very tolerant man but I was allergic to my next door neighbour. She said she'd be on my drive at 1 pm sharp and did I prefer red or white. I said I preferred tea and then she asked if that would be green or herbal. I said it would be PG Tips but I could tolerate Yorkshire Tea if essential.

Part 16

Mother used to say some days were trapped wind and some were wet farts. She said that about most weekends, and especially Christmas, Easter and Bank Holidays. Every day the post office wasn't open, thinking about it. I know she used to like sitting behind the counter even on her days off but I always assumed that was because she had bottles filed away in various places. I was always intrigued as to why Lambrusco ended up with passport applications but she explained the logic – it was because you needed a passport to get to Italy. She had gin stashed with car tax for some reason though and the Christmas brandy was with commemorative stamps. Not a system I'd have thought of personally but I have to say it worked for her. Trapped wind days usually ended with her under the counter by tea-time singing "Show me the way to go home". Wet fart days ended much the same way but never lasted much beyond midday and she'd always finish with Mack the Knife.

Rotating the tins felt a bit rushed today but Octopus was arriving so I might have to just straighten up one or two of them tomorrow. I love knowing I can go shopping on a Friday with a list in my hand. The wife never made a list. She said she shopped on impulse. I asked if that meant you came back with a bag full of ingredients we'd never use. She used to roll her eyes when I said things like that. Told me we could sometimes deviate from the list of daily meals I'd first drawn up when we got married and that's why she always bought a few different ingredients – just in case one day I decided to spice things up a bit more. I said that was unlikely and she agreed it was and went for one of her lie-downs.

She was bored with the monotony of our meals, she said; told me that once she dreamed of serving up sausage and mash on a Wednesday instead of its normal Tuesday just to see my face. But that was around the same time as threatening to mix up the contents of all my organiser tins so I put it down to a menopausal flush and a fit of pique. I'd actually thought I was helping out by taking the responsibility of having to decide what to cook every day. I remember mother throwing a tin of custard over some Spam one night because father complained he didn't want beans on toast again. She called it Spam Surprise. And then there was the time she put corned beef on top of shredded wheat, drizzled it with brandy and said it was loosely based on a dish from French Provincial Cooking by Elizabeth David. Father didn't complain about the beans after that. I didn't mind the shredded wheat one actually but I've never been able to track down the recipe she mentioned.

I did wonder what the neighbours would think when the strange car pulled up on my drive. You don't see many of those in Lesswilling. Most of the time, it's a Scoda or a Peugeot, not a Porsche Boxter. The only problem was that just as she arrived, it started raining. My first reaction was we would have to cancel the picnic but Octopus just shrugged and said a picnic in the living room would be almost as good if we put down the rug she'd brought down on the floor. I wasn't sure my knees were up to getting back up again even if I did manage to get down but she was very persuasive and said she would give me a hand if I got stuck, and not to be so defeatist. Told me plenty people my age took up yoga or Tai Chi and had I considered doing something like that. I explained I had a very full schedule during the week with my planner already full of commitments but she said why fill a week with housework tasks when I could be out meeting other people. By the time we were eating the scones and cream, I'd been persuaded to have a small glass of red wine and to take off my tie.

I did raise the subject of her unusual name after the scones. She said her parents had been marine biologists. She thought it was better than Squid, which her father had suggested, or Mollusc, her mother's preferred choice. I asked whether they had ever considered something like Beryl or Susan, and admitted I'd assumed she was a man at first. She said it was a common assumption but she was very much a woman and what's more, she had a wife who lived in Paris and two children. That threw me. Two children I could understand but the wife bit was confusing. I know some ladies do prefer other ladies but she didn't look like one of them. But then again, I don't suppose I've met one before. You don't get them in Lesswilling, I'm sure. She had mentioned she was a Guardian reader though and there aren't many of those either. They only stock one in the newsagents and that's for Timmy Timmons who tells everyone he once voted Socialist Worker before he went Lib Dem.

I did ask why she was being so helpful to me over the divorce and she told me that the story of my wife's bottom imprinted in paint on the wall had brought back memories of when she went home one day and found her then long term partner entertaining the window cleaner and the postman on their kitchen table. I said that must have been a dreadful experience but far better to have seen it than eat her breakfast there the next morning totally unaware. She said she hated infidelity and duplicity, and I agreed, making a mental note to check the meaning of duplicity later. Octopus said it had been that experience which had convinced her to specialize in divorces and it had been the best decision she'd ever made; it was far more interesting than conveyancing, she said. There was nothing exciting about stamp duty and reckoned such points came along when the cosmos decided we needed to move forwards and make life changes whether we knew it at the time or not. I said I thought the cosmos must have decided I needed a massive kick up the arse what with the wife moving out and that neighbour moving in. Octopus said it was highly likely, the cosmos was always one step ahead of us, that the bigger picture would be revealed to me when the time was right.

I asked if she thought the cosmos had any idea of just how irritating the new neighbour could be. I told her that anyone with any principles would never have done the things he'd done to that garden. She said she liked a person with principles and we agreed that they had become unfashionable in today's society, although I was at pains to stress that here in Lesswilling, we still had them, along with lawns; apart from the bloody neighbour, who had neither. Octopus said she thought she might be able to offer me a little help with that provided my principles didn't get in the way. I said there was a time to stick to your principles and a time when they needed to be applied with a little more flexibility and she told me pragmatism was an intelligent approach. Pragmatism, another word to look up.

She went shortly after that but only after we'd agreed to meet next week. She wants to have more exercise and fresh air and loved the idea of walking in the park. Cheaper than a gym, as I said, which sparked a little idea, but before I put pen to paper, I want to double check my list for tomorrow and I might even add a bottle of wine. It didn't even bother me when I went to look up something on Google and those nuns were still at it because I was too busy thinking about what the cosmos was telling me. Right now I'm thinking, ok, the wife might have buggered off and the new neighbour might be a pillock, but Alan, the world could be your lobster even yet, as mother used to say. I know most people say "oyster" but mother liked to be different and the gin never helped.

Part 17

Sorry for the lack of communication since Thursday but I've been rather more busy than normal. I've been writing a plan for when I get the money from the wife for the house. Octopus had suggested I invest it but Rose said she thought I was too risk averse for stocks and shares. I think "risk averse" is just another way of saying cautious, and I admit I can be cautious. I seem to have spent my entire life being cautious and look where that's got me. Time for this worm to turn, I've decided and to prove it, I've already swapped sausage and mash to Mondays and I've found a recipe for a lamb casserole. The winds of change are on their way, as mother used to say after she'd let rip with a smelly one, before blaming the dog we didn't have.

But before the winds of change arrived, there was the small matter of the week's laundry to see to, so at 10 prompt, I was outside next door with my laundry basket and box of Persil. He looked a bit agitated when he opened the door but told me to go in the utility room and he'd be in to explain how to use the machine. Utility room, indeed; bloody southern inventions coming up here and turning women's heads. The wife had told me they'd got a utility room up in Morewilling. I'd asked what shade of Farrow and Ball she'd be using for

74

that but she just sniffed and said how wonderful it was to live with a man who thought making her happy was the most important thing in life. I told her I'd spent a long time trying to make her happy too but that I'd never seemed to manage it. I'm thinking now maybe even she didn't know what that would take.

I went where he pointed and then stood around looking at photos of him with famous people, like Des O'Connor, her off "Wish you were here" and one of him with Prince Harry, although I dare say that will be quietly dropped very soon, once the memoirs have come out. I suppose if you have to show off, sticking them up in a utility room is as good a place as any. Mother had a photo of her meeting the queen but if you looked, you could see the Sellotape she'd used to stick two pictures together.

He came in, pushed a cup of coffee at me and took out a piece of paper from his pocket. He said it had been through his door early this morning. He thrust it at me to read for myself. It was from a firm of solicitors. "Dear Sir" it began and then went on. "My firm understand you have been somewhat lax in seeking the necessary approvals for the work carried out in your garden at… blah, blah. I hereby give due notice that you are required to remove the offending additions within a time frame of fourteen working days or face a considerable fine… blah blah…" It was signed Octopus Fields.

I said nothing and pushed it back. Best not to let on I knew her, I thought, or I might end up paying at the launderette, so I busied myself packing my dirty washing into his machine. He pressed a few buttons which seemed to start off the washing, and then ran his fingers over his head and said that this was the end for him in Lesswilling. There was no way he could do what was being demanded, and certainly not in that time frame. I agreed that there was no way he could replace the lawn as well, not unless he had it all turfed and that would cost another pretty penny. I didn't particularly want a conversation, especially not this one, but I was a sitting target. *Next time,* I thought, bugger the cost, *I am using the launderette.*

He told me he'd only moved next door after the break-up of his marriage and he'd thrown everything he had into it after his husband had decided to become a monk in Tibet about six months before. He said he'd moved up north to have a fresh start and because everyone had told him northerners were friendly and sociable. I was torn between listening to him and thinking that Lesswilling seemed to be turning into a magnet for homosexuals and wondering if it would affect house sales. Then again, it hadn't harmed Brighton, had it. The wife's cousin said house prices had shot up there faster than they kept adding another letter to LGB. By the time they added the plus sign, you couldn't get a two-bedroom terrace for less than a quarter of a million.

I could see from the display that I had another 45 minutes before I could retrieve my Fronts and bedding and make an escape, so I told him that losing a partner was very traumatic but that perhaps ripping up lawns for Hot Tubs and posh sheds wasn't a long term solution, especially when it upset your neighbours. I said I'd been going through something similar with the wife but that I'd found walks in the park very restful, especially with someone else. He said it would be wonderful to just have a quiet walk with a friend in the park and before you know it, I'd suggested he join me that afternoon and I was telling him about my business idea.

He thought it was a brilliant concept which played to the desire for the simple pleasures in life that many people were going for now and began talking about self-annihilation, or something like that, and a bloke called Maslow. Could have been his husband I suppose but I'm not sure where the annihilation would come in. He did say before he'd retired though, he'd run his own advertising agency and he'd love to help get my idea off the ground. Perhaps he could invest some capital into it. My ears pricked up at that so by the time my laundry was finished, I'd told him not to worry about the letter he'd received – I'd have a word with Octopus. After all, I admitted a bit sheepishly, it had only ever been intended to scare him. That's when he told me he'd been the one to scupper my computer signal and bugger up the internet. Said it had been childish retaliation for my complaints to the council but he'd put it right for me and that, by the way, the council had never got in touch with him. I told him that was because they only had one functioning department and even that needed Viagra.

We've spent a couple of hours this evening in his summer house talking through the plan I'd written. That wind of change was certainly blowing today – I never even thought about my toast and Lurpack at ten. I was too busy deciding on the name of the business. James had suggested it needed to be short and snappy but sum up what the business was about, preferably in no more than three words. He thought Park perambulations was a bit long – winded. In the end, after a bit of soul searching, I decided that correct spellings and accurate syntax weren't as important as a catchy name and even if anyone in Lesswilling did bother to complain, they'd only get put through to the refuse department. So Walkz'n'talkz was born tonight.

Walkz'n'talkz

Enjoy a listening ear and a friendly shoulder as Alan guides you around the beautiful paths and sights of less willing Park. Light refreshments to share; picnic baskets by arrangement.

Leave loneliness behind Make new friends
The new caring and sharing way to be healthy and happy without risky romance

Decide if you prefer one to one conversation or small group interaction and book your time slot. Wheelchairs welcome by prior arrangement.

No expensive gyms, no pricey pubs and no hidden costs. Contact……

I didn't want to add my home number and suddenly realized I would need a mobile phone after all. Barbara had suggested an Apple but I'd feel pretty stupid talking into a phone that looked like a piece of fruit but then I'm not sure about Rose's suggestion of an android. I saw Terminator 1, 2 and 3 and world domination isn't part of my master plan. Not yet, anyway.

Part 18

There's not been that much time recently just to natter. Octopus pushed through the divorce and the settlement on the house and we celebrated that night round at James's next door, along with Rose, Fifi and Barbara. Not in the hot tub, I hasten to add. We remained fully clothed in the summer house although I did leave my tie off.

James and I get on very well now actually. He hasn't erected anything new in his garden for ages; he says he doesn't feel compelled to always be changing things anymore. Says he's quite content as he is although I suspect he's taken a bit of a shine to him who's moved into number 69. I saw them laughing together outside the butcher's last week and James seems to be going there much more than he used to. He's even stopped his supermarket delivery and he must have a freezer full of sausages by now. I suggested we drop off a flyer for the walks through 69's door, just to welcome him and be neighbourly of course. James said that was a very good idea and we could ask the estate agent to include one of our brochures when they handed over the keys on any sale completion. He's very persuasive, is James.

Within a few weeks of going public, I had five investors – James, Rose, Barbara, Octopus and Timmy Timmons who said he was bored with the Lib Dems, disillusioned by socialism and fancied trying capitalism before he shuffled off his mortal coil. I'm not sure what a mortal coil is but another few thousand being invested was very welcome. It meant I could have personalized T-shirts printed for every member of the group. Timmy even changed his morning paper over to the Telegraph which means there are no Guardian readers in less willing now.

It was tempting, I admit, to try to run it all myself but in the end, with the advice of Octopus, I agreed a small team would be far more efficient. We're thinking of putting in for Investors in People next month. James takes care of promotions and sales, Barbara runs the office and bookings from the summer house next door. She does 10:30 till three weekdays and her niece covers filing on Saturday mornings. I do the walking and talking; around the park with a flask and a pack of Shrewsbury biscuits. The picnic baskets have proved to be surprisingly popular. Once a month, Octopus puts on a social event in James's garden with a barbecue and hot tub for all the members and I organise a quiz. They're always very well attended. It's amazing how many people are lonely but just crying out for a bit of companionship rather than wanting the bother of a romantic entanglement. What they do between walks is up to them of course. We're all adults and a discreet liaison, so to speak, keeps the spirits up. Or as Mother said, a lay a day keeps the coffin away. I think once a day is pushing it, personally but Rose, Barbara and I have an arrangement that works for us; not at the same time, you understand.

I had to buy a new weekly planner of course for the bookings. That's my preferred way of keeping track although

Barbara has a proper system with spreadsheets. The old weekly planners are in a drawer somewhere because some things had to go completely and I had to compromise on others. The tins might be facing the wrong way, I admit, but the new automatic washing machine, a slow cooker and someone in to do a bit of cleaning every week have been real time investments. I'm at the stage now where we either need to close bookings or I need to employ another Alan, so to speak. There aren't enough hours in the day with just me now. We can't decide whether to employ another walker or whether to start a franchise, like James suggested. Personally, I'm not keen on the franchise idea myself as I would need to quality assure them. You don't let someone mess up your brand image, do you? Or, as mother used to say, if anyone's going to crap in your back yard, make sure it's you, not some other bugger.

Part 19

I found the old weekly planners this morning. They were in the Plan sideboard which I was clearing out ready for the hospice shop. I've decided the bungalow needs a fresh look and Octopus reckons Plan is very dated now. The mango bathroom is going next month. I'm not having white though – I've chosen something called Porcelana Blanca. And there'll be no bloody bidet either – the salesman said it was considered very European to have a bidet so I reminded him we'd voted Brexit to avoid things like that and us Brits are perfectly capable of using paper.

I had two phone calls tonight. The first was from that Crepuscular Rays, asking if there were any spaces on one of the walks. I told her I was sorry but her destiny would not ever include Walkz'n'Talkz. When she asked why, I just told her to pack off. Having a Twix in the car for my tea that night still rankles. The other call was just after six thirty. It was the ex-wife. She said she'd left it until after six to avoid interrupting my tea. I'd not eaten yet, I said, so could she hurry up as I didn't want the risotto to go dry. She asked what had happened to the six o'clock news and since when did I eat risotto. I said not living with a menopause had been liberating for me too and could she get on with why she'd phoned.